When they were children, Queen Elsa and Princess Anna's parents often told them bedtime stories. One night, their father told them a story about the Enchanted Forest where the Northuldra people lived.

Long ago, Arendelle and the Northuldra people went to war with each other.

The girls enjoyed the story, but they had a lot of questions about what happened, so Queen Iduna soothed them to sleep with a special story.

"When I was little, my mother would sing a song about a special river called Ahtohallan that was said to hold all the answers about the past, about what we are a part of," Queen Iduna explained.

Elsa couldn't help but wonder if the mystical river also held answers about her magic powers.

Years later, with their parents
no longer around, Anna and Elsa
spent a lot of time with their best
friends Kristoff, Sven and Olaf.

One night, as the five of them
played a game of charades, Elsa
appeared distracted. Anna was
worried about her and, later that
evening, she went upstairs to
check on her.

"You're wearing mother's
scarf," said Anna. "You do that
when something is wrong."

Elsa assured her sister that she
was fine but, secretly, something
was bothering her. Someone – or
something – was calling to her...

Disney
FROZEN II

 AUTUMN
PUBLISHING

That night she continued to hear the voice and she started to wonder if it belonged to someone magical like her. She followed the voice out of the castle to the fjord. Elsa started to use her powers and she shot out an enormous blast that created ice crystals and showed her the Enchanted Forest.

Suddenly, there was a bright flash of light from the north and the wind stopped, fires died out and the fountains and waterfalls dried up!

Then, Grand Pabbie and the trolls rolled into Arendelle. The wise troll knew about the voice Elsa could hear. They both understood that she needed to head north to the Enchanted Forest and follow the voice. He also told Anna that she must go with her sister.

"I won't let anything happen to her," promised Anna.

Olaf, Kristoff and Sven joined Elsa and Anna and they all headed north. When they reached the Enchanted Forest, they found that an eerie mist surrounded it.

Elsa reached for Anna's hand, the mist parted and they were all able to step inside. Then, the mist closed around them.

As they took in their surroundings, a strong wind swept through the forest, picking them up and flying them round and round.

It was the Wind Spirit and it soon took notice of Elsa's special powers. Then, it forced everyone, apart from Elsa, out of the vortex.

To slow the vortex down, Elsa used her powers to create snow, which turned into beautiful ice sculptures. Each one captured a different moment in time.

Suddenly, they were surrounded by the Northuldra and Arendellian people that were in Elsa and Anna's childhood bedtime story! Still at odds after so many years, they bickered between themselves. Then, they started to close in on the group, but Elsa stunned them all by using her special powers.

"That was magic. Did you see that?" asked one of the Arendellian soldiers, Lieutenant Mattias.

As the two sides continued to argue, a bright flash of fire appeared. The Fire Spirit dashed around the trees, setting them ablaze. Using her magic, Elsa discovered that the Fire Spirit was actually a cute salamander. Elsa's coolness appeared to settle him and he snuggled down in her hand.

Then, Elsa heard the voice again and, as she turned towards it, she noticed the salamander also responding to the voice.

"You hear it, too? Somebody's calling us. Who is it? What do we do?" Elsa asked the salamander.

The salamander hopped out of her hand and ran up a rock. He looked into the distance and then at Elsa.

"Okay, keep going north," said Elsa.

Later, everyone gathered in a forest clearing to enjoy some food and drink.

Anna chatted with Mattias and learned a lot about her father while Honeymaren, one of the Northuldra, explained that the symbols on Elsa's scarf represented the four spirits – air, fire, water and earth.

Then, Honeymaren pointed out a fifth spirit. "Some say they heard it call out the day the forest fell," she said.

"My father heard it," said Elsa. "Do you think that's who's calling me?"

"Maybe," replied Honeymaren. "Alas, only Ahtohallan knows."

Elsa was now even more certain that she had to follow the voice.

Elsa wanted to leave immediately and follow the voice, but Anna didn't want to go without Kristoff. He was busy helping the Northuldra with their reindeer and Anna had no idea when he would return. Anna knew that she couldn't let Elsa go alone and she set off with her sister and Olaf.

When they reached the top of a hill, they gasped at the sight below – it was the wreck of their mother and father's ship! The sisters realised their parents had been searching for the magical river, Ahtohallan, when they disappeared.

"They were looking for answers about me!" gasped Elsa.

Determined to finish the search her parents had started, Elsa vowed to find the mysterious Ahtohallan river. She knew it meant she would have to cross the dangerous Dark Sea. She also knew that it was a journey she would have to do alone, despite Anna begging her not to.

Then, before Anna could stop her, Elsa created a path of ice and formed a boat under Anna and Olaf. Elsa then sent the pair zipping down the ice towards a stretch of water.

"What are you doing? No!" cried Anna.

Anna quickly tried to change the direction of the boat but, instead, it ended up in a river. Olaf and Anna were now drifting along in the boat past the sleeping Earth Giants, while Elsa continued her risky journey north, alone.

Elsa finally reached the Dark Sea. To try and cross the fearsome water, she froze one of the huge waves before sliding down it, but then an even bigger wave knocked her into the sea.

An enormous horse, the Water Nokk, emerged from the water and started throwing her around. Elsa used her magic to create an icy bridle, swinging onto its back.

At first it tried to throw her off but, before long, the two were charging through the huge waves together towards the sandy shore.

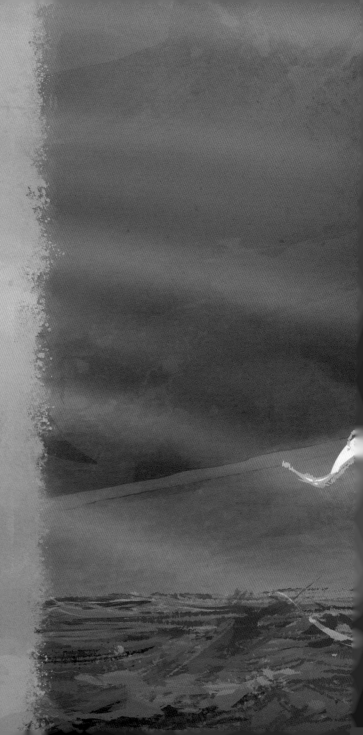

Once safely across the
Dark Sea, Elsa removed the
bridle from the Water Nokk.
Her journey was at an end!
    Finally, the mysterious voice
that Elsa had been hearing for so
long became quieter. Suddenly,
just as the words of her mother's
lullaby had promised, everything
became crystal clear. Elsa knew
she had followed the right path
and she was where she was meant
to be.
    The journey had changed her
and she felt peace. Elsa had no
doubt that the Enchanted Forest
and all the people trapped inside
would soon be free, too.

Across the sea, Anna and Olaf had reached a cavern. Suddenly, an ice sculpture began to form before their eyes. Anna was relieved to see it as she knew it meant Elsa had made it across the Dark Sea.

Anna looked closely at the ice sculpture in front of them.

"I know how to free the forest," gasped Anna. "I know what we have to do to set things right."

Anna took a step forward. It was time to free the forest and mend their broken kingdom...